WE WERE TIRED
OF
LIVING IN a HOUSE

LieSeL MoaK SKorpen • Joe Cepeda

G. P. PUTNAM'S SONS

We were tired of living in a house.

So we packed a bag with sweaters
and socks,
with mittens
and earmuffs.

And we moved to a tree.
We liked our tree.

There was always a breeze in the afternoon
that rippled through our roof.
Above in a branch lived a speckled bird
who sang all day for the sake of a song,
and our roof in the autumn turned scarlet and gold.
We liked our tree,

until we tumbled out.

So we packed our bag with sweaters
and socks,
with mittens
and scarlet leaves and gold.

And we moved to a pond.
We liked our pond.

We built a raft and floated about
among the reeds and lily pads.
Below fish darted,
dragonflies above.
And pond frogs sang with us on summer nights.
We liked our pond,

until we sank.

So we packed our bag with sweaters
and socks
and scarlet leaves and gold
and a frog who was a particular friend.

And we moved to a cave.
We liked our cave.

We slept on beds of cool green moss.
We hunted for blackberries in the wood.
We dipped our water from a brook
and roasted walnuts over a fire.
When we weren't busy,
we explored.
We liked our cave,

until we met the bears.

So we packed our bag with sweaters
and scarlet leaves and gold
and a frog who was a particular friend
and precious stones that caught and held the sun.

And we moved to the sea.
We liked the sea.

We built a castle on the shore
of salty water and warm sea sand
with turrets and towers and moats about.
We hunted for treasure and dove in the waves
and slept to the pleasant songs of the surf.
We liked our castle on the shore,

until the turn of the tide.

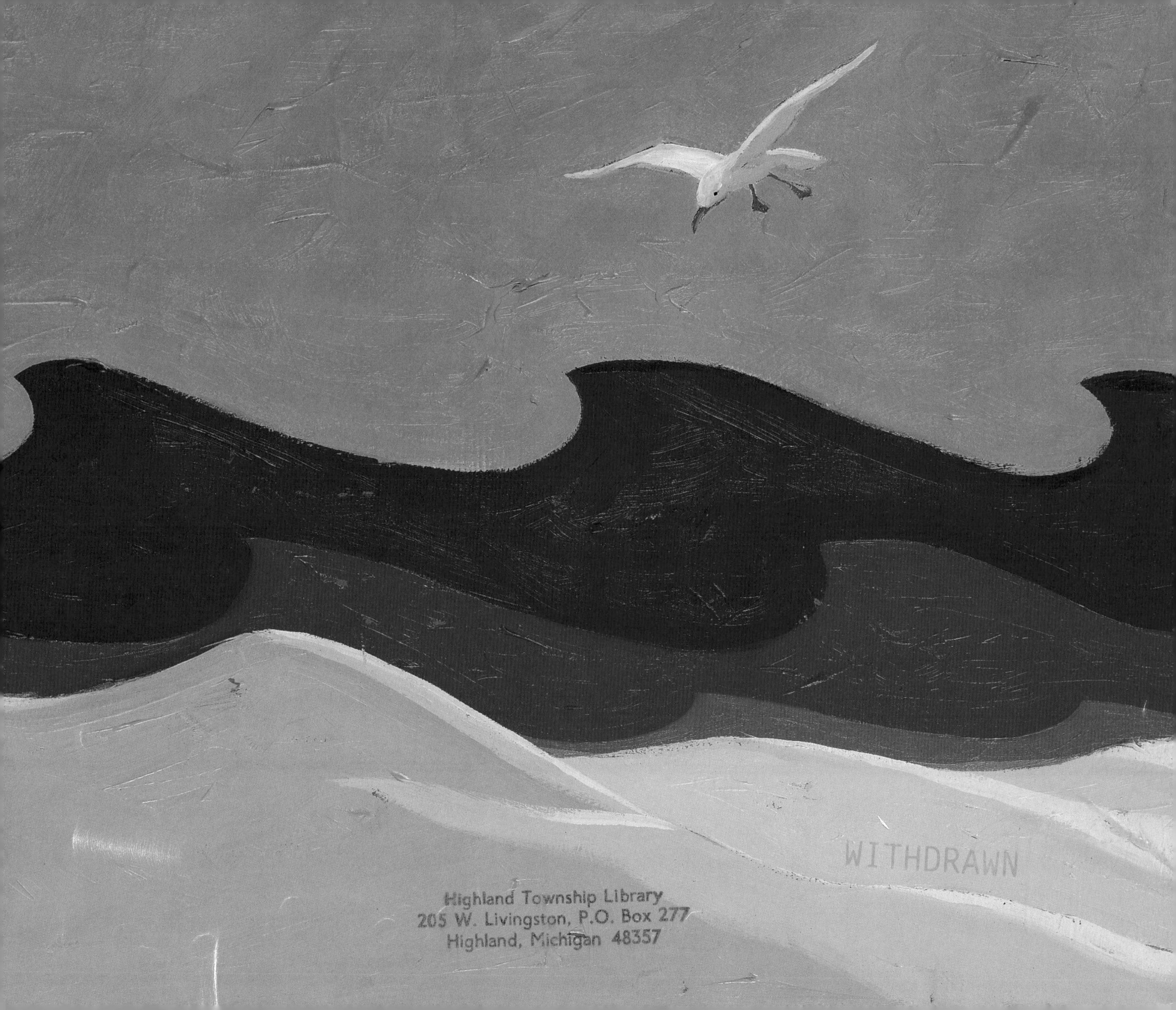

So we packed our bag with scarlet leaves and gold
and a frog who was a particular friend
and precious stones that caught and held the sun,
and seashells singing the songs of the surf.

And we went home to live in a house.

For Samuel Charles Elmes,
Hanna Skorpen Claeson,
Per Skorpen Claeson,
Kate Elizabeth Elmes,
and Benjamin Skorpen Claeson

—L. M. S.

For my brother and sister,
Cesar and Adriene

—J. C.

G. P. Putnam's Sons, a division of Penguin Putnam Books for Young Readers, 345 Hudson Street, New York, NY 10014. G. P. Putnam's Sons, Reg. U.S. Pat. & Tm. Off. Originally published in 1969 by Coward, McCann & Geoghegan, Inc., New York. Published simultaneously in Canada. Printed in Hong Kong by South China Printing Co. (1988) Ltd. Designed by Marikka Tamura. Text set in Cooper Oldstyle Light. The art was done in oil on illustration board. Library of Congress Cataloging-in-Publication Data. Skorpen, Liesel Moak. We were tired of living in a house / Liesel Moak Skorpen ; illustrated by Joe Cepeda. p. cm. Summary: Four children move to a tree, a raft, a cave, and finally the seashore, enjoying each new dwelling until they discover its drawbacks. [1. Dwellings—Fiction.] I. Cepeda, Joe, ill. II. Title. PZ7.S62837We 1998 [E]—dc21 97-14529 CIP AC ISBN 0-399-23016-5

1 3 5 7 9 10 8 6 4 2

First Impression